Robert and the Three Wishes

3 WISHES

Also by Barbara Seuling

Robert and the Three Wishes

3 WISHES

by Barbara Seuling

Illustrated by Paul Brewer

A
LITTLE APPLE
PAPERBACK

SCHOLASTIC INC.
New York Toronto London Auckland Sydney
Mexico City New Delhi Hong Kong Buenos Aires

"Thief" from *Storm Coming!,* text copyright © 2001 by Audrey B. Baird. Published by Wordsong/Boyds Mills Press, Inc. Reprinted by Permission.

Special thanks to my good friend Audrey Baird for writing "Guess Who It Is?" (pages 9–10) exactly the way she believed Robert would write it.—B.S.

ISBN 0-439-35377-7

Text copyright © 2002 by Barbara Seuling.
Illustrations copyright © 2002 by Paul Brewer.

12 11 10 9 8 7 6 5 4 3 2 1   2 3 4 5 6/0

Printed in the U.S.A.
First Scholastic printing, April 2002

To my wonderful writers' group—Bonnie Bryant, Miriam Cohen, Sandra Jordan, Peter Lerangis, Ellen Levine, Fran Manushkin, Harry Mazer, Norma Fox Mazer, and Marvin Terban—for their support, love, and laughter
—B. S.

For Gary, Aline, and Cyrus
—P. B.

Contents

The Contest

Robert rolled his pencil back and forth as Mrs. Bernthal talked.

"Class, I received a very interesting letter," said Mrs. Bernthal, "from *The Instant Millionaire* show."

Robert stopped the pencil in mid-roll and looked at his best friend, Paul, who sat on the other side of the table. Paul looked back at him and shrugged.

"*The Instant Millionaire* show!" shouted Lester Willis. Lester Willis always called out without raising his hand.

1

"Yes," said Mrs. Bernthal. "*The Instant Millionaire* show."

"Wow!" said Emily Asher. Everyone turned to look at her. Emily Asher almost never called out. She probably couldn't help herself. *The Instant Millionaire* show was the most popular show on TV. People won a million dollars for answering questions correctly.

"I don't know how they got my name," Mrs. Bernthal said with a smile.

Robert wiggled in his seat. He had sent in a postcard to *The Instant Millionaire* show with Mrs. Bernthal's name on it. She was the smartest person he knew. He couldn't be a contestant himself because you had to be eighteen years old to be on the show. He had told Paul about sending the postcard. Paul looked like he was squirming in his seat, too.

"Unfortunately," continued Mrs. Bernthal, "I can't be a contestant on that show.

I have a cousin who works for the TV station, and there's a rule. Close relatives of employees cannot be on their game shows."

Robert relaxed. At least Mrs. Bernthal wasn't mad. "I like contests," she went on. "They are lots of fun, and they encourage you to think. Since you are the best class in the whole school, I'm going to let you have a contest of your own. It will be a week from Monday. That will give you time to prepare."

"Yeah!" shouted Joey Rizzo. "For a million dollars?"

"Oooooh!" squealed Melissa Thurm.

"Cool!" said Brian Hoberman.

"It will work just like the TV show, except for the money, of course," said Mrs. Bernthal. There were a few groans. "We'll use points instead. The boys will be one team, and the girls will be the other." She asked them to choose captains for their

3

teams. The boys chose Paul. The girls chose Emily Asher.

"Mrs. Bernthal, what's the prize?" asked Vanessa Nicolini.

"The prize?" repeated Mrs. Bernthal, looking a bit surprised. "Oh, that's true. Contests always have prizes, don't they?"

"Yes! Yes!" said the children.

She stopped for a moment to think. Robert wished they could just have a big party at the end. Then nobody would have to be a winner or a loser. Winning was fun, but losing a contest could make you feel awful. And Susanne Lee Rodgers, the smartest kid in the class, was a girl.

"The team that wins gets to throw a class party," said Mrs. Bernthal.

Robert almost fell off his chair. That was just what he was wishing for!

"The winners can choose their own decorations, music, party games, and treats," Mrs. Bernthal said. "Whatever you like."

The class clapped and shouted, "Hurray! We're having a party!" Lester Willis whistled. Mrs. Bernthal tried to frown at him, but she was still smiling.

Robert sat at his desk, frozen in place. Wow! Wait until Paul heard about this. He made a wish and it came true!

Getting Spooky

Paul frowned when Robert told him about getting his wish. "That's weird," he said.

"I know." Robert took the salami out of his sandwich and ate it. Then he ate the cheese and threw the bread away.

"We could use a little magic to win this contest," said Andy Liskin. They were all sitting at the same lunch table. "The girls have Susanne Lee on their team."

"I have all the books in the *Weird & Wacky Facts* series except for #23," said

Robert. "You can all borrow them. If we memorize the facts, maybe the boys can beat the girls."

The boys looked doubtful, but agreed to try.

After lunch, Robert sat down at his table and took out his math book with the brown cover. They always did math when they got back from lunch.

"I wish we could just skip math for once," he whispered across the table to Paul. Paul smiled in agreement.

Mrs. Bernthal took out a book with a shiny blue cover. It was not their math book. Robert looked at Paul. Paul stared back at Robert. "You're really getting spooky!" he whispered. Robert swallowed hard.

Mrs. Bernthal opened the book. "This poem is called 'Thief.' It's by Audrey B. Baird." She read:

Like the Sandman,
Storm Man
slips through the night,
a bag of rain
on his shoulder.
Wind gusts
from his nostrils!
Lightning flashes
from his fingers!
Thunder crashes
when he opens his bag!

And, like a thief,
Storm Man steals slumber away.

Robert could not believe it. As Mrs. Bernthal talked, explaining how the author wrote a poem to express her feelings about a storm, Robert looked at Paul. Paul's eyes were bugging out. He whispered, "Wish for no homework." Then he laughed.

Robert laughed, too. It *was* kind of funny. Twice in one day, he'd gotten what he wished for. He had never been this lucky before.

For the rest of the afternoon, the class wrote poems. Robert's poem was about Sally, the class snake.

Guess Who It Is?
by Robert Dorfman

There is a girl in my class I like a lot.
Melissa, Kristi, and
Susanne Lee it's not.

She is the best girl in school.
She is really, really cool.

She doesn't giggle or
talk all the time.
She never, never feels like slime!

Here is a clue.
She is like a worm, only longer.
Like a hose, only shorter.
I like her best when
she makes her S.

Did you guess?

Yes!

I'm in charge of Sally the Snake.
I even feed her when she is awake.

Everyone would like this job, I bet.
Because Sally Snake is
a great class pet.

Robert liked the way the words wiggled on the page like Sally did.

On the way home, he and Paul talked about the contest.

"We're going to have to work extra hard to win this contest," said Paul.

"I know," said Robert. "It's going to be hard to beat the girls. Susanne Lee knows everything!"

"At least you and I have read all the *Weird & Wacky Facts* books," said Paul.

"If the rest of the boys read them, maybe we can win," said Robert.

"Remember to bring some in on Monday," Paul said.

"Okay. If only Susanne Lee wasn't in the contest," said Robert, "we would at least have a chance."

Paul nodded in agreement. They walked the rest of the way home without saying anything.

Special Powers

On Monday, Susanne Lee was out sick.

"Uh-oh," said Paul. "Your wish came true."

"What wish?"

"On Friday, you said if only Susanne Lee wasn't in the contest, the boys would have a better chance at winning."

"That wasn't a wish," said Robert. Or was it? He didn't wish for her to be sick. Was it the same thing?

Paul smiled and shrugged. "Just joking," he said.

Robert knew he was having some weird luck lately. First he wished for a class party, and he got his wish. Then he wished they could skip math, and they did. And now maybe he got another wish, even if he didn't mean for it to be one.

"She's probably got swollen tonsils or something," said Paul, trying to comfort Robert. Paul knew about that because he was out a few weeks ago when his tonsils were swollen. "She'll probably be back in class tomorrow."

Robert sure hoped so. This was making him nervous. It was like he had special powers or something.

He couldn't stop worrying the whole rest of the day. He worried all through dinner and that evening, too. He phoned Paul.

"What if I do have the power to make someone sick?" he said.

"Why? Did another wish come true?"

Paul was beginning to sound really inter-
ested.

"No, but I'm afraid to open my mouth,"
said Robert.

"You can't keep your mouth closed for-
ever," said Paul. "Just don't make any more

wishes. Promise. Cross your heart and say, 'I will not make another wish.'"

Robert thought that was good advice. With his hand over his heart, he said, "I will not make another wish. I promise."

Jail

Susanne Lee was out sick the next day, too. Mrs. Bernthal said Susanne Lee's mother had called. Susanne Lee had a very bad cold and might be out for several days. "It would be nice if you all made get-well cards. I will see that they are delivered to her," said Mrs. Bernthal.

Several days. How many was that? Three? Four? Could she still be out on Monday, the day of the contest?

Robert took a piece of yellow construction paper. Yellow was a good color for a get-well card. It was like sunshine. Robert wished he could feel as cheerful as the yellow paper. He felt gray. The color of a cement block. Cement blocks reminded him of jail.

He wondered if he could go to jail for making Susanne Lee sick. He'd be the youngest person there, probably.

Paul was hunched over his get-well card. It was orange. There was a rainbow on it and a spaceship. Paul always drew spaceships. He was a good artist. Robert had one of Paul's spaceship drawings on the wall of his room. Paul had almost thrown it out, but Robert had rescued it.

"Some ten-year-olds have gone to prison," he told Paul.

"Really?" Paul looked up from his drawing.

"Yes," said Robert. "I saw it once on television." Paul thought about that for a second, then went back to his drawing.

"If I go to prison, I might not see my mom or dad—or even Charlie—for a long time. And Mrs. Bernthal would probably forget me."

"You won't go to prison," said Paul.

"How do you know?"

"You're only eight. You were never in prison before. You never did anything illegal. I

19

don't think they can put you in jail unless you have a record."

"What kind of record?"

"It's like a report that shows if you did a crime before." Paul was rubbing some eraser dust off his paper and deciding which color to use next.

Robert wondered about the time in the park when he dropped a candy wrapper on the sidewalk by mistake. He thought he had tossed it into the wastebasket, but it must have bounced off the edge of the basket and landed on the ground. A park attendant saw it and yelled at him for littering and asked him his name. Robert told him. Could the attendant have reported Robert to the police? Could you go to jail for littering?

"Well, what if I do go to prison? I could grow old in jail. Maybe my mom would come visit me with chocolate-covered jelly cookies. But it would only be for a few minutes, and we would have to talk through a glass window, on telephones. I saw that on TV. Would you write me letters?"

"What? Oh, sure." Paul was startled out of his concentration.

"What will happen to Fuzzy and Flo and Billie?" Robert had a pet-sitting service, and his tarantula, Fuzzy, and the doves, Flo and Billie, had been given to him by people who couldn't take care of them anymore. He had promised he would take good care of them.

"Stop thinking like that," said Paul. "You're being gloomy. You are not going to jail. Just don't make any more wishes."

"Well, okay, but if I did go to jail, would you take care of Fuzzy and Flo and Billie?"

"Sure," said Paul.

Paul was a good friend. Robert felt better.

Robert folded the yellow construction paper and took out green and orange markers. Inside the card, he drew a bird singing. He even drew in a music note near the bird so you would know it was singing. He wasn't sure if the little round part on the note went in front of the line, like a *d*, or behind it, like a *b*. He made it like a *b* and colored it in. He wrote:

TO SUSANNE LEE,
FROM ROBERT D.,
I'M SORRY YOUR SICK,
GET WELL QUICK.

As Mrs. Bernthal walked around the room, she saw Robert's card and corrected it to read:

TO SUSANNE LEE,
FROM ROBERT D.,
I'M SORRY YOU'RE SICK,
GET WELL QUICK.

"Very nice, Robert," she said.

Robert drew a picture of a box of tissues on the front. He remembered how important tissues were when he had a cold. Still, something was missing.

"Take your cards home to finish them," said Mrs. Bernthal. Robert put his inside his loose-leaf notebook to take it home with him.

Breaking the Spell

Robert's mom was making a cup of tea in the kitchen when he got home.

"Hello, Rob," she said. "Did you have a good day?"

"Uh-huh," he said, putting down his book bag and unzipping it. He took out the card he had made for Susanne Lee and showed it to his mom.

"That's very nice, Rob," she said. "I like the box of tissues."

"Thanks," Robert said. His mom could always see what he was trying to draw.

Melissa Thurm had looked at his card in school and asked him why he'd drawn an iceberg on his get-well card.

He opened the kitchen drawer, where his mom kept a box of cough drops. He took out three cough drops and wrapped them in a piece of aluminum foil.

"What are those for?" asked his mom.

"They're for Susanne Lee. She has a cold."

"Oh," said his mom.

Upstairs, in his room, he taped the foil package to the card. Then he took a tissue from the box near his bed and cut a little square out of it and glued one end of it to the box of tissues. It looked like a tissue was popping out of the top of the box.

Now the card was ready to send. He put it back in his book bag to take to school tomorrow.

Robert lay in bed staring at the ceiling. He thought about people in stories who were granted wishes. Sometimes things turned out all right, like in "Thumbelina" when the old woman wanted a child and got her wish. But there were other times when wishes backfired, like in "The Fisherman and His Wife," when the fisherman's wife got too greedy and asked for more and more until finally everything was taken away and she was back where she started, with nothing.

Robert got up and turned on the light. He took out his book of fairy tales. Let's see. To break a spell, you had to kiss a frog. No. You had to be a princess for that one. Another story said you had to slay a dragon! No way. There were no dragons in River Edge, New Jersey. He turned out the light and went back to bed.

As he lay there, Robert remembered *The Wizard of Oz*. He had just seen the movie on TV for the second time. Dorothy had to get the broom from the Wicked Witch of the West to go back to Kansas. Robert didn't see how he could do anything like that.

Then Robert thought of something else. The people in the fairy tales got three wishes, max. They never got more than three. Maybe that was the limit on wishes. Robert had had three wishes. He used one wish on the party. He used another wishing the class would skip math. And he used the third—he took a deep breath—on wishing Susanne Lee would not be in the contest.

And now it looked like that one was coming true! Maybe his powers were all used up!

The only way to know, of course, was to make another wish. But he'd promised he wouldn't. He had to talk to Paul.

One More Wish

"**I** have to make one more wish," said Robert.

"You promised!"

"I know. But the only way I can tell if the spell is broken is to make another wish. If it doesn't come true, then we'll know everything is back to normal. Nobody ever has more than three wishes in stories. Maybe I don't have to worry anymore!"

"Hmmm," said Paul. "Okay. But you have to be very careful. Don't do anything yet. After school, I'll come over to your house."

"Great." Robert couldn't wait.

The day seemed to crawl by, but finally the bell rang. Paul walked home with Robert and called his mother from there. "I'm over at Robert's," he said.

The boys sat together in Robert's beanbag chair, where they did their best thinking.

"What should I wish for?" asked Robert.

"You can wish for the phone to ring," Paul suggested.

"It might be someone we don't want to talk to," said Robert.

"Good point." Paul settled down to think again.

"I think we need a snack first," said Robert. His stomach had growled twice already.

"Hey! I have an idea!" said Paul.

"What is it?" asked Robert.

"You know how your mom never has good kid food in the refrigerator?"

"Yeah." Robert's mom kept cookies in the cupboard, and sometimes chips, but the stuff in the refrigerator was usually gross, grown-up food. And sometimes the milk was not too fresh because she forgot to buy a new container before the old one went bad.

"Okay. Let's wish for great food, then."

Robert liked that idea. He was starving. "Blueberry pie," he said. The last time he was at Paul's house, Mrs. Felcher had given them blueberry pie that she made herself.

"Brownies," said Paul, licking his lips.

"Chocolate milk," added Robert.

"Marshmallow-fudge, chocolate-chip, peanut-butter ice cream," said Paul.

"Pizza!"

"Cupcakes!"

Their mouths were watering as they thumped down the stairs.

Robert opened the refrigerator door. They found a bunch of carrots and a container of yogurt and something in a clear wrapper that could be bread.

After a moment, Robert shouted, "Hurray!" and spun around. Paul was there, ready for a high five.

"Congratulations!" Paul said. "The spell is broken!"

Robert took some cookies down from the cupboard. "In a way, I'm sorry," he said.

"Why? Did you want blueberry pie that badly?"

"No, it's not that," said Robert. "I figured if I still had wishes, I could wish for Susanne Lee not to be sick."

"Yeah," said Paul.

Quietly, the boys went upstairs to do their homework.

"The Person I Admire"

Robert had to admit, he felt a little sad not having his special powers anymore. The contest was coming up on Monday. The boys were all reading *Weird & Wacky Facts* books, hoping to get an edge. But nobody knew yet whether Susanne Lee would be back in time to be on the girls' team. It was tempting to think about making a wish to win.

"Susanne Lee thanked you for all the cards and poems you sent her," said Mrs.

Bernthal. "She said they really cheered her up. She has them taped to her bedroom wall so she can see them and think of you. She misses you and being here and hopes to be back with you soon."

Paul gathered the boys together at recess. "Don't worry," he told them. "We're okay, whether Susanne Lee comes back in time for the contest or not. Keep reading. I'm sure we can win."

At lunch, the boys spouted facts to one another.

"An armadillo always has four babies at a time, all girls or all boys," said Brian Hoberman.

Matt Blakey jumped in with the fact that people once believed that horseradish was a cure for headaches.

"Hi, boys," said Emily. "Are you ready for the contest?"

"Emily!" cried Joey. The boys snapped

to attention. "Um, yeah, we're ready. How about you?"

"We're in good shape," said Emily. "Good luck. May the best team win." She left, carrying a big load of books in her arms. She was probably memorizing all kinds of facts, too.

After math, Mrs. Bernthal told the class to get out their notebooks and write about someone they admired. "It could be a famous person, like a president, or an inventor, or an explorer."

"What about Martin Luther King, Jr.?" asked Emily Asher.

"Martin Luther King, Jr., is fine," said Mrs. Bernthal.

"Can I do Frankenstein?" Lester Willis shouted out.

"Frankenstein is the name of the doctor who created the monster. Is that who you mean?"

"No," said Lester. "I want to write about the monster."

"You admire the monster?"

"Yeah. He's cool." Lester Willis looked truly happy with his idea.

"Well, yes, I guess so, then," said Mrs. Bernthal. "You can also write about one of your parents or grandparents, or an uncle or aunt you especially admire."

"How about a teacher?" asked Vanessa Nicolini.

"Why, yes," said Mrs. Bernthal, blushing. "A teacher would be fine."

Robert wrote about Susanne Lee Rodgers. He wrote:

I ADMIRE SUSANNE LEE RODGERS BECAUSE SHE IS VERY SMART.

Robert thought about how she had helped him when he was in the lowest reading group. When she said, "That's very good, Robert," it made him grind his teeth, but she did help him move up to a higher reading group.

He wrote:

I ADMIRE HER FOR GETTING 100 ON ALL HER SPELLING TESTS.

Actually, she got 100 on *all* her tests, except one time when she got one math problem wrong and nearly cried.

He wrote:

I ADMIRE HER BECAUSE SHE HAS A WATCH THAT CAN TELL WHAT TIME IT IS ALL OVER THE WORLD.

Finally, he wrote:

I ADMIRE SUSANNE LEE BECAUSE SHE SAID NICE THINGS TO US EVEN THOUGH SHE WAS SICK.

Then he added in a hurry:

I'M SORRY SUSANNE LEE IS SICK AND IT'S MY FAULT. I HAVE THESE SPECIAL POWERS AND WISHED SOMETHING TERIBLE. IT WAS AN ACSI—DENT. I DIDN'T EVEN NO I HAD THEM UNTIL IT WAS TO LATE.

There. He'd said it. Robert wondered how he could make it up to Susanne Lee. He realized he was grinding his teeth.

The Secret Is Out

As Robert took his seat the next morning, he sensed there was something new in the classroom. The essays they'd written yesterday were graded, and some were hanging on the bulletin boards around the room.

Robert's eyes stopped on his own essay, tacked up on the bulletin board on the coat closet door. It had a red B+ on it. That was the first time ever that he'd gotten more than a B in Mrs. Bernthal's class.

As they put away their jackets and book bags, the children read some of the essays.

"Hey, Robert," said Matt. "Can you make me fly?"

"Um, the spell is over," Robert answered.

"That's too bad," said Kristi Mills. "I thought you could make it be summer vacation."

"Well, um, I'm sorry." Robert felt a bit like he was the toothpaste in a tube that was being squeezed.

"Don't worry about it, Robert," said Paul. "They'll get over it."

"Class," said Mrs. Bernthal, clapping for everyone's attention. "Your contest will be on Monday. You have all weekend to get ready. Be sure to put on your thinking caps before you leave your house on Monday morning."

Mrs. Bernthal always talked like that. She told them they had to wear their thinking caps, and even drew one on the board with a lightbulb on it. "The lightbulb," she said, "is to show that the person wearing the cap is thinking."

Paul reminded the boys during recess what their team's strategy would be. "Think before shouting out an answer," he said. Paul looked right at Lester when he said it.

"Okay," said Lester, grinning.

Paul continued, "If you aren't sure what the question is, ask Mrs. Bernthal to repeat it." The boys nodded.

Finally, Paul said, "Don't listen to what the girls say. They will try to make us nervous, but it's just to scare us."

"And we're doing a good job of it, too," said Abby Ranko, startling them. The boys spun around.

"A spy!" said Joey.

Abby laughed again and walked away.

"I wish Robert still had his powers," said Matt.

"Me, too!" said Kevin Kransky.

Me, too, Robert thought.

Pep Talk

Robert's stomach did a flip-flop when he walked into the classroom on Monday morning. Susanne Lee was back. It was great to see she was all right, but it meant the boys would lose the contest now.

"Robert, can't you try your powers, just in case?" asked Joey.

Robert explained, "Even if I still had my powers, which I don't, I wouldn't use them. They can get people into trouble."

"Yeah," said Matt, "but we need help to win the contest."

Robert didn't argue with Matt. It was no use. Everyone thought having special powers was such fun.

"Hey, guys," said Paul, jumping in, "you memorized all those facts in the *Weird & Wacky Facts* books. Maybe we'll win. And if we win, we'll have a great party with gummy worms, and vampire teeth, and

those cans of green slime we can spray on one another." Robert admired Paul for giving the boys a good pep talk.

"Yeah!" said Lester.

"Ee-yew!" said Susanne Lee, coming up behind them. "That stuff is gross!"

"Hey, Susanne Lee. How are you feeling?" asked Andy.

"I'm fine, thank you," said Susanne Lee.

"Hi," said Robert. "I—I'm glad you're better."

"Thanks, Robert," said Susanne Lee. She looked at Matt. "It's important to work hard for what you want. Then you'll know you earned it."

Robert almost felt his teeth grinding. Then he remembered how glad he was that Susanne Lee was not sick anymore, and he felt better.

"Are we ready to begin?" asked Mrs. Bernthal.

"YES!" said the class all at once.

"Okay, then," said Mrs. Bernthal. "Let's begin!"

"It's now or never," whispered Paul. Robert tried to smile.

The Best Party

"There are nine boys and eleven girls," said Mrs. Bernthal. "Boys, you line up over here on this side of the room." She pointed to her left. The boys scrambled for places against the chalkboard wall.

"And girls over there," said Mrs. Bernthal, pointing to the opposite side. The girls went to their places, against the supply cabinets.

"I will give each side a question," said Mrs. Bernthal, holding a sheet of paper. "You may talk over your answer with your teammates, if you wish. If your final answer is correct, your team will get one point. After each side has answered twenty questions, we'll count up the points. The team with the most points is the winner of the contest."

The children were buzzing with talk, eager to begin. They got quiet as Mrs. Bernthal read the first question to the boys.

"Which President of the United States weighed more than three hundred pounds?"

Paul, as captain of the boys' team, was first. He turned to the other boys and whispered. "I think I know it!" he said. Andy nodded. The others nodded, too.

"William Howard Taft," said Paul.

"That's correct," said Mrs. Bernthal. "One point for the boys."

The girls' first question went to Emily Asher.

"What is the largest island in the

world?" asked Mrs. Bernthal, moving to the next question.

Emily turned to Susanne Lee and the other girls. She wasn't sure. Susanne Lee whispered to her. Emily turned to Mrs. Bernthal and said, "Greenland."

"That is correct," said Mrs. Bernthal. She made a mark on her score sheet.

The questions went pretty quickly. The score was almost even for a while. Then the boys missed two in a row. The girls applauded whenever the boys got an answer wrong. Robert felt his confidence slipping, even though he had answered two questions correctly.

Paul tried to cheer the boys up with another pep talk. "Come on, guys, we can do it! Don't give up. We can't let the girls beat us."

The girls did win, in the end. The boys were good sports, though, even if they could not count on having green slime at the party.

Emily Asher made a victory statement, thanking the boys for a good contest. Then she invited them all to the girls' party tomorrow. She said she was sure they would enjoy it, even if there were no vampire teeth. The boys groaned.

Susanne Lee got up to say her mother would make cupcakes for everyone, with pink frosting on them.

"What about gummy worms?" asked Lester.

"Oh, boys are so gross," said Melissa Thurm, walking away.

Robert and Paul looked at each other.

"Don't you wish you had another wish right now?" asked Paul.

"You bet!" said Robert, imagining Melissa Thurm finding a bag of real worms. "But I promised. No more wishes."

"Right!" said Paul, giving Robert a high five.

BARBARA SEULING is a well-known author of fiction and nonfiction books for children, including several books about Robert. She divides her time between New York City and Vermont.

PAUL BREWER likes to draw gross, silly situations, which is why he enjoys working on books about Robert so much. He lives in San Diego, California, with his wife and two daughters.